Barbie™

Fun To Make

Activity Book

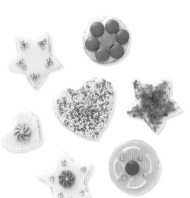

DK

A Dorling Kindersley Book

DK

Dorling Kindersley

LONDON, NEW YORK, SYDNEY, DELHI, PARIS,
MUNICH and JOHANNESBURG

Senior Designer Sarah Ponder
Designer Tanya Tween
Text by Cynthia O'Neill
Senior Editors Cynthia O'Neill, Marie Greenwood
Managing Art Editor Jacquie Gulliver
Senior Managing Editor Karen Dolan
DTP Designer Jill Bunyan, Susan Wright
Production Jo Rooke
Photographer Steve Shott
Prop designer and modelmaker Katie Sheffer

First published in Great Britain in 2000
by Dorling Kindersley Limited,
9 Henrietta Street, London WC2E 8PS

2 4 6 8 10 9 7 5 3 1

Colour reproduction by Media Development, UK
Printed in L Rex, China

Barbie fun to make activity book.-- 1st American ed.
p.cm.
   Summary: Instructions and photographs for projects
such as making paper flowers and jewelry, featuring
special tips from Barbie.
   ISBN 0 7894 5333 9
1. Handicraft--Juvenile literature. [1. Handicraft.]
1.Title: Fun to make activity book.

**The publisher would like to thank the following for their kind
permission to reproduce their photographs:**
Telegraph Colour Library: Bavaria – Bildagentur 43, right;
Bluestone Productions 43, left.

Dorling Kindersley would like to following for their help in making this book:
Ashleigh Frost, Danielle Bromley, Emily Couchman, Esther Templer,
Georgia Richfield, Gregg Richfield, Hannah Mead, Hannah Partridge,
Harriet Forbes Lange, Jessica McKenzie, Katelyn Birchmore,
Lily Dang, O'Shea Pascal, Serena Dwyer, Stephanie Joannou,
Tiffany Simpson, Victoria Cheroomi.

For our complete
catalog visit
www.dk.com

Contents

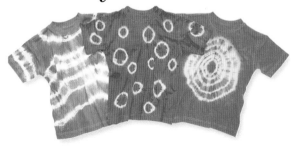

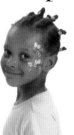

Starting off

Hi there! Are you ready to have fun? Because this book is packed with ideas for things to make and do! Inside, you'll find brilliant designs for jewelry, yummy things to eat and drink, and wonderful gifts to make your friends! Step-by-step photos and simple instructions take you through each stage of the activity. And photos of the things you need for each project are shown at the beginning, so you can gather everything together. It's easy, when I show you how – so let's get started!

Barbie™

A collection of paints, pens, and stickers will always come in handy!

The colored sequins and gems you need can be found at most craft shops

Stationers and big department stores sell many types of paper and card

Golden rules

No matter which project you are trying out, remember to follow the golden rules! It's the best way to make sure you get the most fun from every page!

Before you start any activity, read the instructions all the way through.

! Be careful! Don't use sharp knives or scissors unless a grown-up is there to help you work safely.

Keep clean! Wear an apron, tie back long hair, and always wash your hands before you cook!

Work at a wipe-clean surface, or put newspaper down on the table before you start an activity.

Junk jewelry!

It's easy to create fantastic jewelry from household junk. All you need is a little imagination! Read on to learn how to turn foil wrappers into a sweetheart pendant, or spare buttons into a colorful necklace. There's even a clever idea for turning the lid from a dish-detergent bottle into a glittery ring, with a secret compartment!

You will need

Pipe cleaners

Safety scissors

Sequins

Foil or plastic candy wrappers

Cotton swabs

Cardboard

Felt-tip pen

Glue stick

Ribbons, at least 20 in long

Sweetheart pendant

1 Draw a heart shape, about 4 in across at the widest point, onto thick cardboard. Cut it out.

2 Flatten out the candy wrappers. Cut them into 1 in squares – take care not to tear them!

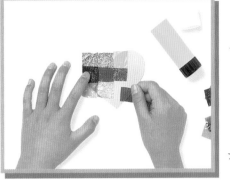

3 Glue the squares of candy wrapper onto the cardboard heart to make a checked pattern.

4 If the squares of foil overlap the edges of the heart, fold them over neatly and stick them down on the back.

5 Bend a pipe cleaner so it is the same size and shape as the heart. Glue it to the cardboard.

Barbie says:

Always take care when you are using scissors!

6 With a cotton swab, dot a little glue onto a sequin. Glue a sequin neatly in the middle of each square, to finish off.

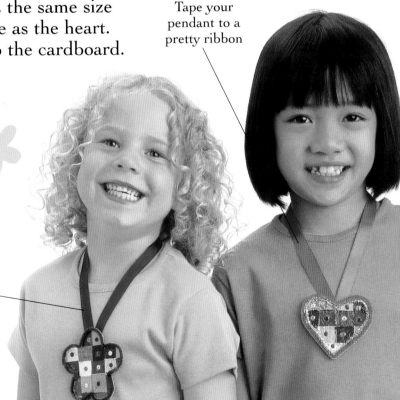

Tape your pendant to a pretty ribbon

Why not try different shapes, like this flowery pendant?

Secrets ring

Glue

Small photo of a pet or friend

Craft ring

Dish-detergent bottle lid

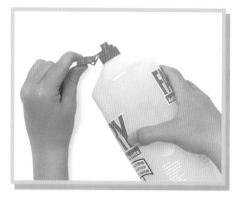

1 Pull the lid from an old dish-detergent bottle (you may need to ask a grown-up for help).

2 Put the lid on top of thin cardboard and draw around it. Cut out the circle you have made.

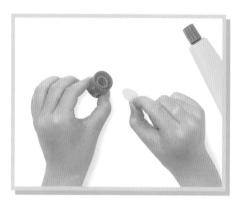

3 Glue the cardboard into the bottom of the dish-detergent bottle lid. (The cardboard should fit tightly.)

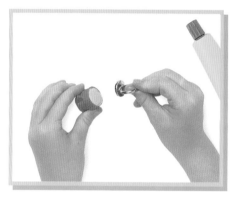

4 Now put a drop of the strong glue onto the flat top of the craft ring. Stick the ring to the cardboard inside the lid.

5 Decorate the top of the lid-ring with a glittery or flowery sticker.

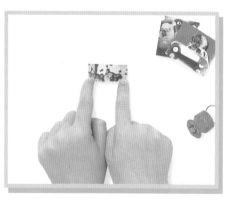

6 Fold the small picture into a thin strip, then slip it inside the secret compartment of the ring. Now it's ready to wear!

Only you will know the secret!

Bright as a button!

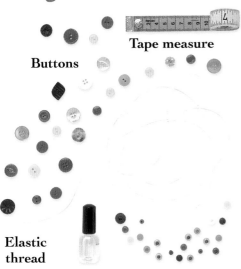

Buttons

Tape measure

Elastic thread

Nail polish

Beads

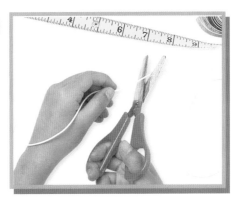

1 Measure around your neck. Cut some elastic thread, three times longer than this measurement.

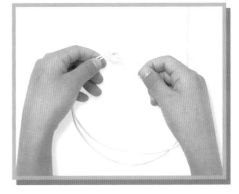

2 Fold the elastic in half. Tie a knot in the folded end, to make a small loop, as shown here.

3 Paint the cut ends of the elastic with clear nail polish. This will stop them fraying and make it easier to thread the beads.

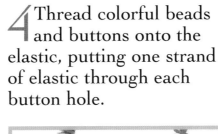

4 Thread colorful beads and buttons onto the elastic, putting one strand of elastic through each button hole.

Barbie says:

Make a button bracelet, too. Use a shorter length of elastic thread and follow steps 2 to 6!

5 Build the buttons and beads into a multi-colored design, until you have almost reached the end of the elastic thread.

6 Knot the loose ends and put the knotted end through the loop. Tie this. Slip the necklace over your head.

Terrific tiara

I feel like a princess in a fairytale when I wear a tiara. Now you will, too, when you make the terrific tiara on these pages! It's covered with spangles, glitter, and stars, and is perfect for a special occasion, a fancy dress party, or just dressing up with your friends. And the best thing about this tiara – it's fun to make!

You will need

Strong glue

Pen

Mirrored card

Safety scissors

Glitter glue pens

Gems

Loose sequins

Strings of sequins

Strings of fake pearls

Tape measure

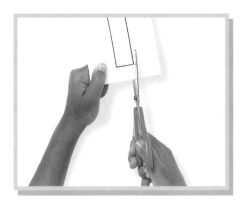

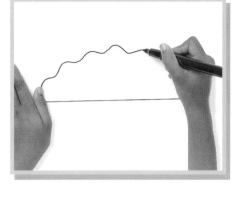

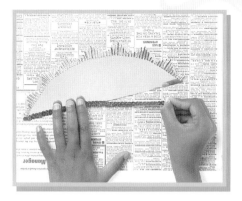

1 Cut out a long strip of mirrored cardboard, about 1 in wide and 24 in long. Put this to one side; you will need it later on.

2 Draw a front for your tiara, measuring about 8 in x 3 in, on the back of the mirrored cardboard. Cut out the shape.

3 Use strong glue to stick sequins and beads in a pretty pattern over the front of the cardboard.

Fit for a Princess

4 Once the glue is dry, put more glue on the back of the card. Stick it to the long strip.

You may need to bend the tiara to the shape of your head

5 Glue the ends of the strip together, so that the tiara will sit snugly on top of your head.

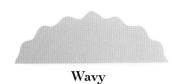

Tiara styles

You can change the style of your tiara by cutting out different shapes. Here are some of my favorites.

Spiky

Smooth

Wavy

Flower power

You can make beautiful presents or cards, or create a pretty secrets diary, by pressing the flowers and leaves that grow in your garden. It's simple, when I show you how! Remember, the easiest flowers to press are the ones with flat faces – pansies or flat-faced roses are just right.

You will need

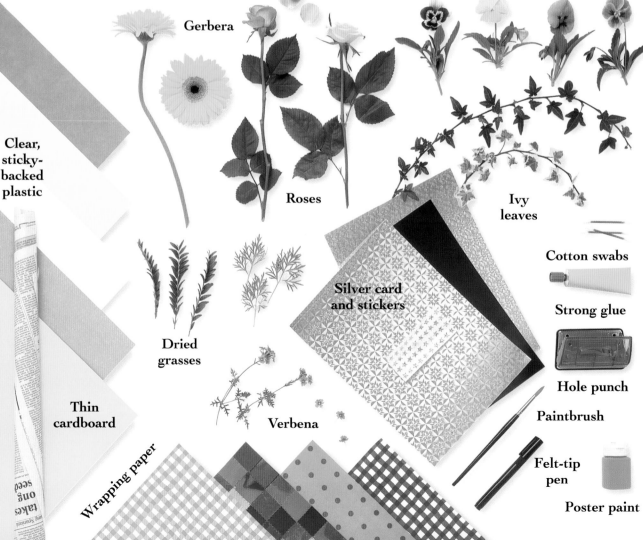

A mix of flowers, such as here

Gerbera

Clear, sticky-backed plastic

Roses

Ivy leaves

Cotton swabs

Silver card and stickers

Strong glue

Dried grasses

Hole punch

Thin cardboard

Paintbrush

Verbena

Felt-tip pen

Wrapping paper

Poster paint

Pressing fresh flowers

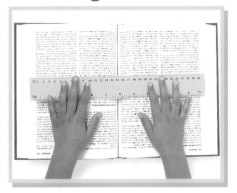

1 Find a heavy book (a dictionary is good). Measure the width and height of the open pages.

2 Cut a piece of blotting paper to the size of the open pages. Lay the folded paper on the book.

3 Choose the mix of flowers you want to press. Snip off the stems with some safety scissors.

Barbie says:
Make sure you leave the flowers to dry for at least four weeks!

4 Lay flowers and leaves on top of the blotting paper. Only use the right-hand side of the book.

5 Arrange flower petals elsewhere in the book. Close it, and stack a pile of heavy books on top.

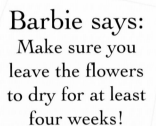

Beads

Safety scissors

Ruler

Long satin ribbons

Heavy books

Blotting paper

Ribbon

Colored writing paper

Once you've piled the heavy books on top, leave your flowers to press for one month

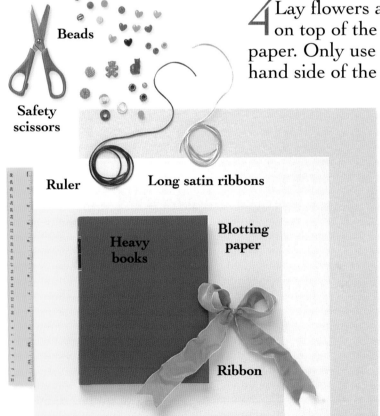

Bookmark

14

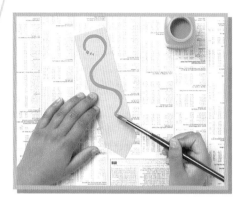

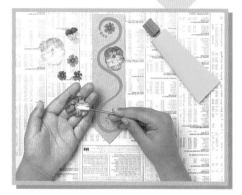

1 Draw a strip, 5 x 2 in, onto cardboard. End it in a point, like an arrow, and cut it out.

2 Use watercolor paints to begin your design. Why not start it with a stem and some leaves?

3 With a cotton swab dab glue on the pressed flowers. Stick to the cardboard in a pattern.

These flowery bookmarks make pretty gifts for friends and relatives!

4 To protect the flowers, cover the bookmark with clear sticky-backed plastic, measuring about 7 x 3 in.

5 Glue your flower design onto a piece of silver cardboard.

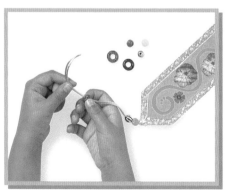

Use the ribbon to fix the tag to your gift

6 To finish off your bookmark, make a hole in the tip. Thread a ribbon, strung with beads, through the hole.

Keep your design simple

Barbie says:
Adapt these steps and use a small square of cardboard to make a special gift tag!

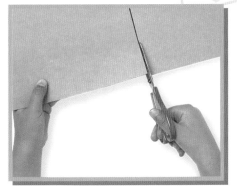

1 Choose two pieces of pretty cardboard. Cut each one to measure about 12 x 8 in.

2 Line up the cardboard. With a hole punch, make two holes in the left-hand side of each piece.

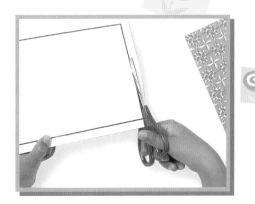

3 Cut some silver cardboard, 10 x 6 in. Glue to one of the bigger pieces of cardboard.

4 Make a flower picture. Stick pressed flowers and petals onto plain cardboard. Why not use stickers or beads, too?

5 When your design is finished, cover the picture with a piece of clear, sticky-backed plastic to protect it.

6 Glue the flowery picture to the front cover of your diary.

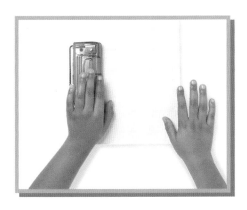

7 Make the inside pages by cutting rectangles of paper just smaller than the covers. Punch holes in the side of the pages.

8 Put the paper inside the covers, with the holes lined up. Tie ribbons through the holes, to hold the book together.

Pretty braids

Trying a new hairstyle is great fun. Here is one of my favorite ways to create a completely different look – pretty braids!
Follow these simple steps to make a basic braid. Then you can have a wonderful time trying lots of new styles, like the ones I've shown on the next page. And here's a great Barbie tip – ask a friend to help you. It's more fun with two or three!

You can choose from

Hairbands

Slides

Flower-shaped hairbands

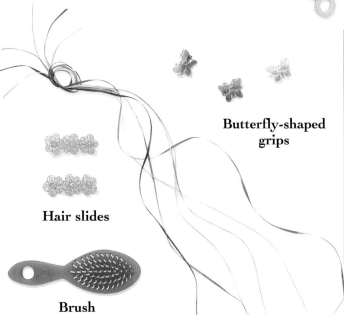

Butterfly-shaped grips

Hair slides

Brush

Comb

Ribbons

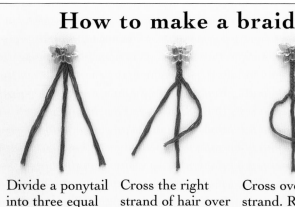

How to make a braid

Divide a ponytail into three equal strands.

Cross the right strand of hair over the middle strand.

Cross over the left strand. Repeat last two steps to end.

Basic braids

1 Comb the hair and pull it into a ponytail (don't pull too tight!). Divide the ponytail into three strands.

2 Lift the right strand. Cross it to the middle, between the other strands of hair. Pull it firm.

3 Cross the left strand into the middle. Repeat 2 and 3 until all the hair is braided. Tie with a band.

Now try these!

1 Make three thin braids on each side of the head. Keep them in place with clips and ribbons.

2 Put the hair into two bunches and braid them. Pin to the back of the head for a fun look!

3 Wind a ribbon around one of the strands of hair before you braid it, for an extra-pretty look!

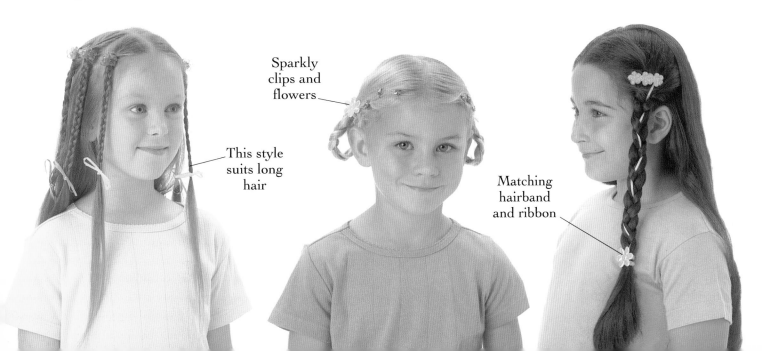

Sparkly clips and flowers

This style suits long hair

Matching hairband and ribbon

Forever flowers!

Here's a bouquet of flowers that will bloom all year round! Pop these paper flowers into a vase (without water!) to brighten up your bedroom with a splash of color. Or why not make a big bouquet as a fabulous gift for Mother's Day?

You will need

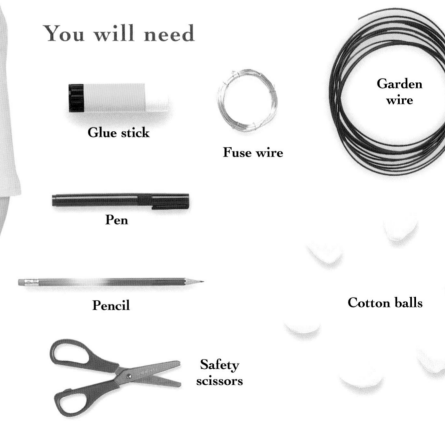

Glue stick

Fuse wire

Garden wire

Pen

Pencil

Cotton balls

Safety scissors

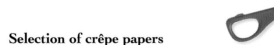

Selection of crêpe papers

Delightful daisy

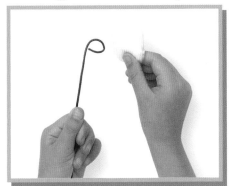

1 Take a 12 in length of garden wire. Make a loop at one end and glue a cotton ball to the loop.

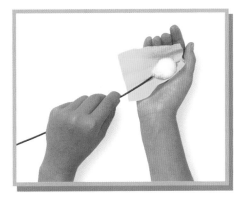

2 Cover the cotton ball with a square of crêpe paper, 3 x 3 in. Glue it around the cotton ball.

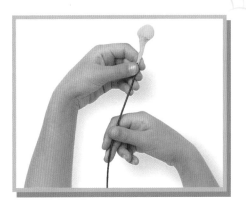

3 Twist any leftover paper around the garden wire for a neat finish, and glue it down.

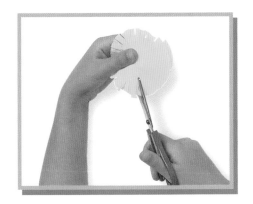

4 Cut out two crêpe paper circles, each about 3 in across. Snip around the edges, making a fringe about 1 in deep.

5 Thread the fringed circles on the wire stem. (See page 48 for a tip on how to make small holes in paper.)

6 Finally, wrap 4 in of fuse wire tightly around the wire stem and the base of the petals, to hold them together.

Paper circles

It's easy to draw a circle on crêpe paper. Just trace around a mug, can or small saucer, then cut it out!

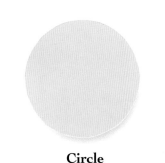

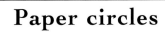

Circle

Try lots of colored paper – bright yellow and blue for a funky mix!

Pretty in pink – pale colors look sweet!

Sunshine yellow and orange look cheerful together

Pretty posy

1 Take a sheet of pink crêpe paper, 8 x 6 in, and fold it in half to make a double thickness.

2 Enlarge and copy the posy shape on page 21 onto the top of the paper. (See the tip on page 48.)

3 Cut around the flower outline through both sheets of paper to end up with two flower shapes.

4 Thread the deep pink flower shapes onto a readymade stem (turn back to steps 1 to 3, on page 19, for instructions).

5 To hold your flower together, wind 4 in of fuse wire tightly and neatly around the petals and the yellow centre.

Barbie says:
Cover a tubular cookie tin with colored paper to make a vase for your paper posy!

Leaves

1 Draw a leaf, 4 in long, on folded paper (copy shape on page 21). Cut it out, making two leaves.

2 Cover one leaf with glue. Lay a piece of fuse wire, 6 in long, down the middle.

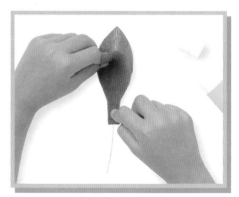

3 Stick the second leaf on top, covering up the wire. A little fuse wire will be left over.

Finishing off

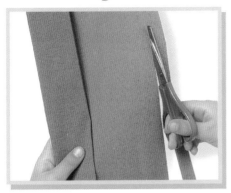

1 Cut out a long, thin strip of green crêpe paper. It should measure around 1 x 20 in.

2 Place the green strip on newspaper to protect your table. Then cover the strip with glue.

3 Fix two leaves to the base of each flower, by winding the leftover fuse wire around each stem.

Separate the paper layers to show off the petals

Pretty posy with stem and leaves

4 Wrap the strip of green paper around the leaves and the stem, until any wire is covered up. Trim the ends neatly.

A colorful mix of delightful daisies and pretty posies!

Flower patterns

Trace and enlarge the shapes below, using the tips shown on page 48. Use them as patterns for the flowers and leaves.

Posy   **Leaf**

Party time!

Next time you give a party, why not make the invitations, decorations and party hats yourself? The day will be even more special if you choose a theme for each guest. Last year, Stacie received a butterfly shaped party invitation from her friend, Janet. At the party, Stacie was thrilled to have her own butterfly picture-straw to drink from and a butterfly hat to wear!

Come to my **party!**

You will need

Colored cardboard and paper

Satin ribbons

Pom-poms

Pipe cleaners

Gift ribbons

Compass and pencil

Safety scissors

Straws

Sticky tape

Glue stick

Aerosol-can lid

Felt-tip pen

Paints

Water

Envelopes

Paintbrush

Pencil

Ruler

Party invitations

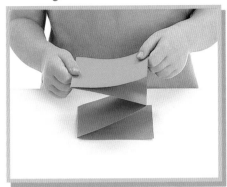

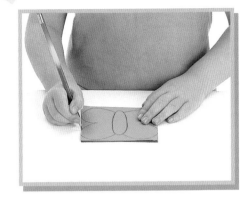

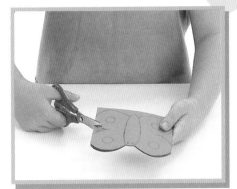

1 Fold a strip of paper, about 17 x 4 in, in half and in half again. Open and pleat along the folds.

2 Draw a butterfly (or a heart, flower, or other design) on the top pleat of colored paper.

3 Cut out the butterfly – but don't cut around the outline where it overlaps the edge of the paper.

Barbie says:

Your drawing should fill the space and the edges must overlap the edges of your paper!

4 Open out the paper. You should find a line of butterflies! Draw fine details onto each one.

5 Now decorate your invitations with paints or stickers.

Write the details of your party on the back of each invitation

Come to my PARTY!

Picture straws

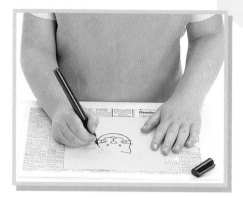

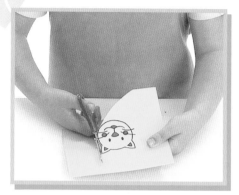

1 Draw around the lid of an aerosol can onto cardboard. Make one circle for each guest.

2 Draw an animal or a cute bug on each circle (pick different designs for each guest). Paint them.

3 Cut out the pictures. With grown-up help, make little slits in the top and bottom of each one.

4 Push a straw through the bottom slit of each picture and out again through the top slit.

Barbie says:
Write the name of each guest on the back of their picture straw, so they know where to sit at the table.

Add wings and stalks to the card circle to make a buzzy bee!

You won't have to draw a circle to create a colorful butterfly

Make delicious party drinks – see the recipes on page 28

Picture patterns

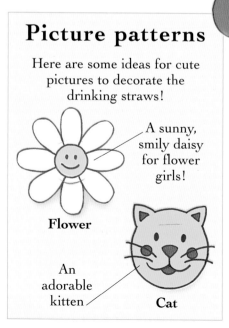

Here are some ideas for cute pictures to decorate the drinking straws!

A sunny, smily daisy for flower girls!

Flower

An adorable kitten

Cat

Party hats

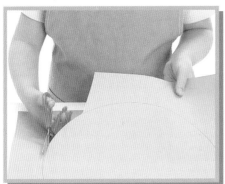

1 Draw a 12 in circle onto cardboard (see page 48). Cut it out, then cut it in half.

2 Bring the edges of the cardboard together to make a cone (leave a gap at the top). Glue down.

3 Run curly gift ribbons through the small gap at the top of your hat and tape to inside of hat.

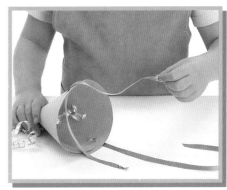

4 Make a small hole on each side of the cone. Thread the holes with silky ribbons and knot these into place.

5 Paint a design on the cardboard (we chose butterflies). Cut out. Stick to the hat with some glue.

Party hat, decorated with tiny ladybugs

Party hat decorated with cute bumblebees

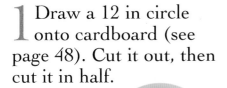

Cute cakes

I always think the best bit of baking a cake is choosing the yummy decorations to finish it off! These mini-cake treats come in all sorts of shapes, and they're so pretty, too! Serve them next time you have a party, or when friends come over after school.

Now let's get started!

You will need

Teaspoon

Dessert spoon

Small bowls

Candies

Flaked chocolate

Candied fruits

Chopping board

Sieve

Cake decorations

Plastic bowl

Family-sized sponge cake

Warm water

Cookie cutters

Food colorings

Confectioner's sugar

1 Using different-shaped cookie cutters, cut lots of mini-cakes from the family-sized sponge cake.

2 Now make glacé icing. Use a sieve to sift the confectioner's sugar into a bowl to get rid of lumps.

3 Slowly add drops of warm water and mix it in. Stop when the mixture is fairly runny, like glue.

4 Divide the icing into some small bowls and mix a few drops of red or green food coloring into each one.

Try using orange juice, instead of warm water, to make an orange flavored icing

Use cake toppings, chocolate, or candies to decorate your cute cakes whichever way you want!

5 Use the icing at once. Spread it carefully over the cakes and leave to set. Then cover your cakes with decorations!

Candy Cake

Orange delight

Chocolate star

Classic heart

Hundreds 'n' thousands

Lemon delight

Silver starburst

Dreamy drinks

Share delicious drinks with your friends when you make these chocolate ice-cream shakes and frothy fruit ices. For extra fun, serve the drinks in pretty glasses, decorated with fruit, cocktail umbrellas, and colorful straws.

Mmm! They're delicious!

You will need

Spoon

Knife

Ice cream

Chopping board

Chocolate sauce

Fruits

Milk

Ice-cube tray

Fruit-flavored juice

Blender

Ingredients

All quantities are to make two drinks, so increase the quantities as necessary.

FRUIT ICE

Selection of soft fruits

Flavored ice cubes, made with fruit-flavored juice

CHOCOLATE SHAKE

16 oz vanilla ice cream

2 tablespoons chocolate sauce

2 cups milk

 NEVER use a blender unless a grown-up is around to help you!

Fruit ice

1 Peel and chop up some soft fruit (try kiwis, grapes, mangoes, or strawberries).

2 Make flavored ice cubes from fruit juice. Blend these in a blender to turn into crushed ice.

3 Put a layer of fruit, then a layer of ice, into a glass. Repeat these layers until the glass is full.

Chocolate shake

1 Put two scoops of ice cream, one spoon of chocolate sauce, and two cups of milk in a blender.

2 Blend the whole mix together until well-blended (about 15 seconds). Pour and serve!

Bendy straw for extra fun!

Sprinkle the shake with flaked chocolate

Barbie says:

For a new flavor, try strawberry sauce instead of chocolate!

Kiwi fruit

Raspberry snow

Keep your cool when the sun is out with this delicious recipe for Raspberry snow! That's what I call these deep-pink ice-pops. They're made from frozen yogurt and raspberries, so they're a healthy treat on a hot day. If you don't like raspberries, try the recipe with strawberries instead. It tastes just as delicious!

You will need

Here's a cool idea!

Ice-pop molds

Masher

Teaspoon

Tablespoon

Plain yogurt

Plastic bowl

Raspberries

Raspberry yogurt

Sugar

Milk

Ingredients

If you are using strawberries instead of raspberries, remember to change the flavor of the yogurt, too!

8 oz raspberries

1 or 2 tablespoons sugar

16 oz raspberry yogurt

7 oz plain yogurt

4 tablespoons milk

1 Wash and dry the raspberries and put them into a plastic bowl. Sprinkle them with sugar.

2 Mash the fruit and sugar into a pink paste, a little like jelly. Try to get most of the lumps out.

3 Add raspberry yogurt and plain yogurt to the plastic bowl. Give the fruity mixture a good stir.

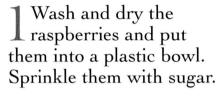

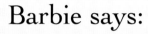

Barbie says:

Always wash your hands and put on an apron before you start cooking!

4 Add the tablespoons of milk to the bowl, and stir them in well.

5 Use a teaspoon to put the mixture into ice-pop molds. Pop these in the freezer for six hours.

Treat your friends! They'll think you're really "cool"!

Tie-dyed T-shirt

Add a splash of color to your wardrobe, and turn a plain white T-shirt into a brilliant new top, when you tie-dye it. Your friends will be amazed by your new look, especially when you tell them you created it all by yourself! This activity is quite messy, so make sure you ask a grown-up before you set to work.

You've got the look!

You will need

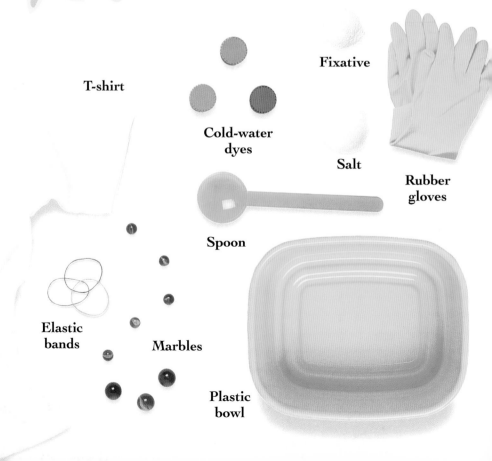

T-shirt

Fixative

Cold-water dyes

Salt

Rubber gloves

Spoon

Elastic bands

Marbles

Plastic bowl

Safety scissors

1 Tie lots of marbles into the front of your T-shirt. Hold each one in place with an elastic band.

2 Now tie marbles into both sleeves, again fixing them in place with elastic bands.

3 Using gloves, soak T-shirt in dye for about an hour (see instructions on pack for exact time).

Barbie says:

Always follow the instructions on the pack of dye!

4 Take the top out of the dye. Rinse in cold water until the water runs clean.

5 Take out the marbles. Iron the top when it's dry – then wear it!

Made with one marble, tied with five bands in a row

Make this top using elastic bands and no marbles

The T-shirts make super presents for your friends, too!

Picture perfect

I love sitting down to make pictures with my little sister, Kelly. Here's a technique we think is really fun – tearing paper into squares to make a colorful mosaic.
You don't need to be especially good at drawing to try this, and you won't need paints, just some old magazines and some glue! Foil candy wrappers make great mosaics, too.

Barbie says:
Don't get sticky glue on the table – protect your work surface with a sheet of old newspaper!

You will need

Newspaper

Cardboard or colored paper

Glue stick

Pen

Ruler

Pages from old magazines

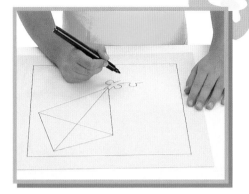
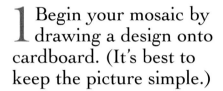

1 Begin your mosaic by drawing a design onto cardboard. (It's best to keep the picture simple.)

2 Choose colors for the picture. Find magazine pages with these colors; tear into small squares.

3 Working from the top and sides, put glue on part of the background; stick on the paper squares.

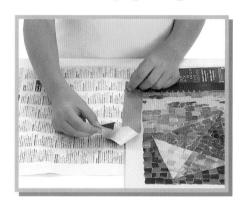

4 Finish the background of your mosaic first, before you start working on the main area.

5 For details such as the string of this kite, put the glue on the paper square, not the cardboard.

6 Make a "frame" by sticking long strips of colored paper around the edge of your mosaic.

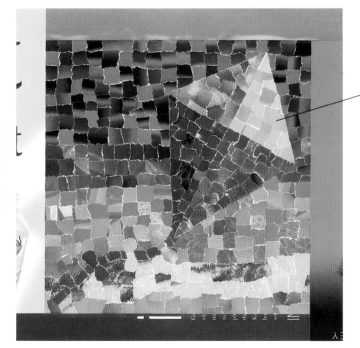

This gorgeous kite is soaring in a deep blue sky

Try different designs, like this beautiful butterfly

Paper magic

Did you know that you can make "pottery" from paper? This "paper magic" is called papier-mâché, and it's great fun! In the next few pages, I'll show you how to use papier-mâché to make colorful plates, and a truly beautiful jewelry box.

You will need

You can make it!

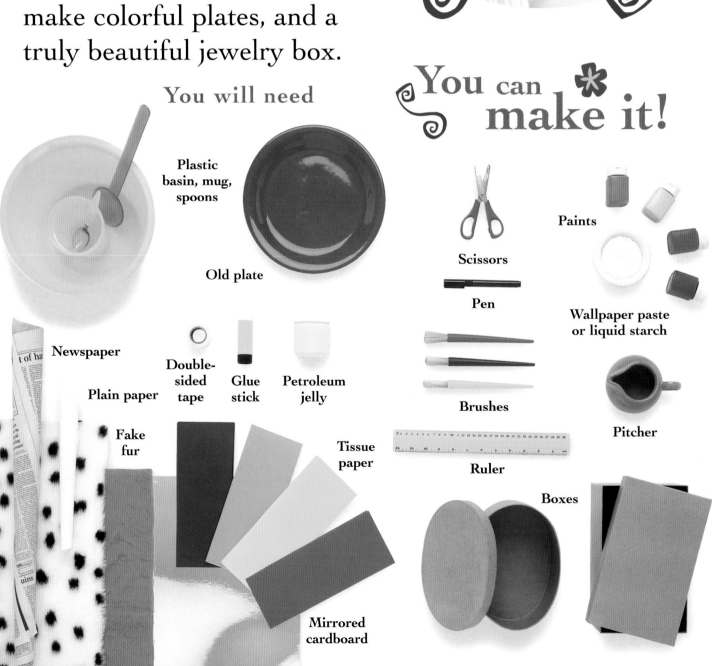

Plastic basin, mug, spoons

Old plate

Newspaper

Plain paper

Double-sided tape

Glue stick

Petroleum jelly

Fake fur

Tissue paper

Mirrored cardboard

Scissors

Pen

Paints

Wallpaper paste or liquid starch

Brushes

Pitcher

Ruler

Boxes

Pretty plates

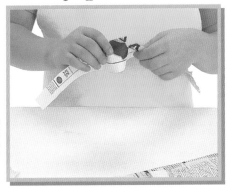

1 Tear sheets of old newspaper into lots of squares, each measuring about 2 in across.

2 Thickly cover a plate with petroleum jelly. (It stops the papier-mâché from sticking to the plate.)

3 Cover the plate with four layers of old newspaper; paint each layer with paste or starch.

4 Finish with a final layer of white paper, painted with paste or starch. Leave to dry in a warm place for at least six hours.

5 Pull the papier-mâché dish away from the plate. Wipe off jelly with tissue.

6 Paste the inside of papier-mâché dish, cover with a layer of white paper and paste, and leave to dry.

7 Decorate the plate with a checked pattern made from torn-up tissue paper by repeating the instructions in step 6.

Decorated with poster paints; paint lighter colors on first

Trim the edge, for neatness

Jewelry box

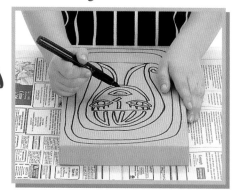

1 Use a marker pen to draw a simple picture of a face in a curvy frame onto the lid of the box.

2 Tear old newspaper into thin strips. Dip in the wallpaper paste and twist them gently.

3 Lay a twist of the newspaper on top of each line of your drawing, until they are all covered.

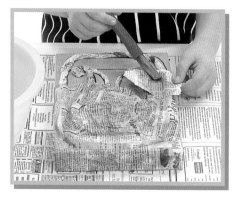

Barbie says:

Protect your work surface – cover it with paper to soak up any mess!

4 To make the eyes, dip balls of paper into the paste. Squash them flat, then stick them down. Leave to dry.

5 When the papier-mâché is dry, cover the lid and the face outline with two final layers of paste-and-paper squares.

Give your jewelry box a touch of glamor by sticking on a string of fake pearls or gemstones

6 Again, wait until the papier-mâché is fully dry, then choose bright colors to paint the box and the face on top.

Just right for jewels!

Finishing off

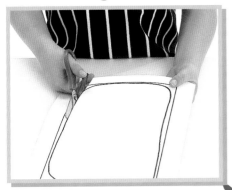

1 Draw around the box, onto the back of some mirrored cardboard. Cut out, inside the lines.

2 Draw a wiggly cardboard frame and stick it to the "mirror," using double-sided tape.

3 Use double-sided tape to stick the mirrored cardboard inside the lid of your jewelry box.

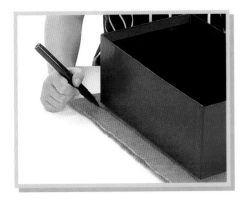

4 With a felt-tip pen or a marker, draw around the base of the box onto the back of some furry fabric. Cut the shape out.

5 Measure the length and depth of each side of the box. Cut out a long strip of fur to fit the sides.

6 Line the sides and base of the box with strips of double-sided sticky tape. Peel off the backing.

7 Stick the fabric, with the fur side out, inside the box. (Stick on the long side strips first, then finish with the base.)

A box of delights!

Trendy tops

How would you like to design your own T-shirt? All you will need is a plain top, some colorful fabric paints, and a little inspiration! Then choose a design and start to draw. If you want to give your top the personal touch, why not paint a very special design on the T-shirt – a colorful portrait of yourself?!

You make it happen!

You will need

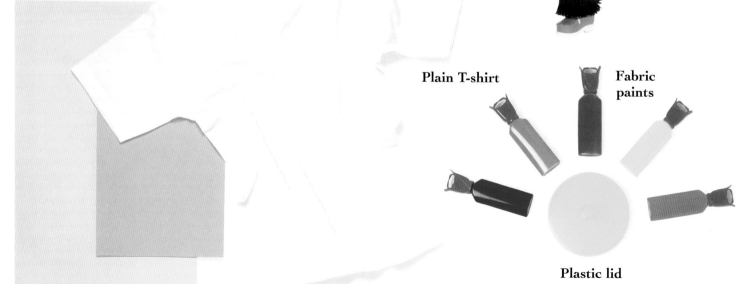

Plain T-shirt

Fabric paints

Plastic lid

Thick cardboard

1 Pull a T-shirt around some card; tape the sleeves back. (It's easier to draw on stretched fabric.)

2 With a fabric paint, draw around a small dish or cookie-jar lid, to make a round, face shape.

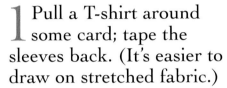

3 Add eyes and a mouth making lots of short, light strokes with the fabric paint.

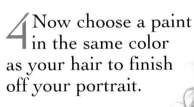

4 Now choose a paint in the same color as your hair to finish off your portrait.

Your self-portrait should contain all those little details that make you unique – from glasses to a bright hair ribbon!

Barbie says:

Ask a grown-up to iron your T-shirt first, so that there are no wrinkles when you paint on it.

T-shirt designs

Try designing a trendy top for a friend or someone in your family. Here are some ideas but don't be limited by them. Use your imagination!

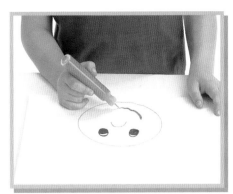

Bicycle

Your dog

Your house

Frame it!

Do you have a favorite photo, one that reminds you of a sunny day? Perhaps it was taken during your best-ever summer vacation or while you were spending a day in the park? Here's how to make a special frame for your super snapshot, to always remind you of the sunshine!

You will need

Fun in the sun!

Newspaper

Bright green crêpe paper

Silk or paper flowers

Cardboard picture mounts

Blue poster paint

Strong glue

Safety scissors

Paintbrush

Fake grass fabric

Ruler

1 Paint the photo mount a bright sky blue (use a sheet of newspaper to protect your work table).

2 When the paint is dry, stick some fake grass (cut to size) to the bottom edge of the photo mount.

3 Cut out strips of green crêpe paper, about 8 x 6 in, and roll them into narrow tubes.

4 Glue along one edge of the stems; stick them to the sides of the frame.

5 Glue silk or paper flowers on the stems (also see pages 18 to 21).

Barbie says:

Make a frame with a beach theme, too! Here's one for you to copy!

Paint on a fluffy cloud

Tape your sunshine photo to the back of the photo frame!

Starfish give a "beach" feel

Sprinkle on glitter when the paint is still wet

This paint has been mixed with a little sand

Kiss and make up

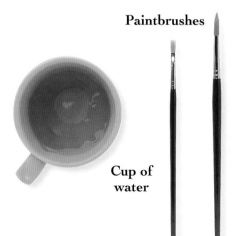

One great way to have fun with your friends is to paint gorgeous pictures on each others' faces. The summery design I show here is a mix of flowers and honeybees! Make sure you buy water-based face paints. They are easy to put on, and they wash off easily, too! And if you have long hair, tie it back – a headband is ideal.

You will need

Water-based face paints

Glitter

Face gel

Paintbrushes

Cup of water

Now let's get **started!**

Barbie says:
Remember to wash your paintbrush between each color!

Why not try these ideas?

Flower   Butterfly   Rainbow   Heart

Flowers

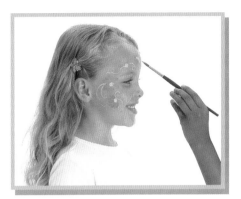

1 With a flat brush, paint yellow circles on your friend's face – these are the middle of the flowers.

2 Paint on some pretty purple petals. Don't forget to wash the brush between each color.

3 Add curly green stalks to link each flower. Finish off with dots of gel mixed with glitter.

Bumblebees

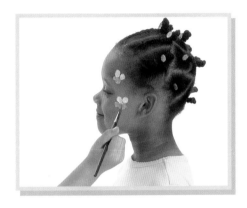

1 Begin by choosing a flat brush to paint small, round bumblebee bodies on to your friend's cheeks or forehead.

2 Carefully draw wing shapes with white paint on each bee. Wash the brush.

3 Use black paint to add stripes, eyes, and little stalks onto your bee.

4 Paint tiny white spirals under your bee, to make it look as if it is buzzing through the air!

Friendship bracelets

Show your friend how much she means to you, by making her a friendship bracelet. All you need are some beads and some strands of wool – choose them in your friend's favorite colors, or to match her best outfit! I'll show you how easy it is to weave the strands together and thread the beads. Have fun!

You will need

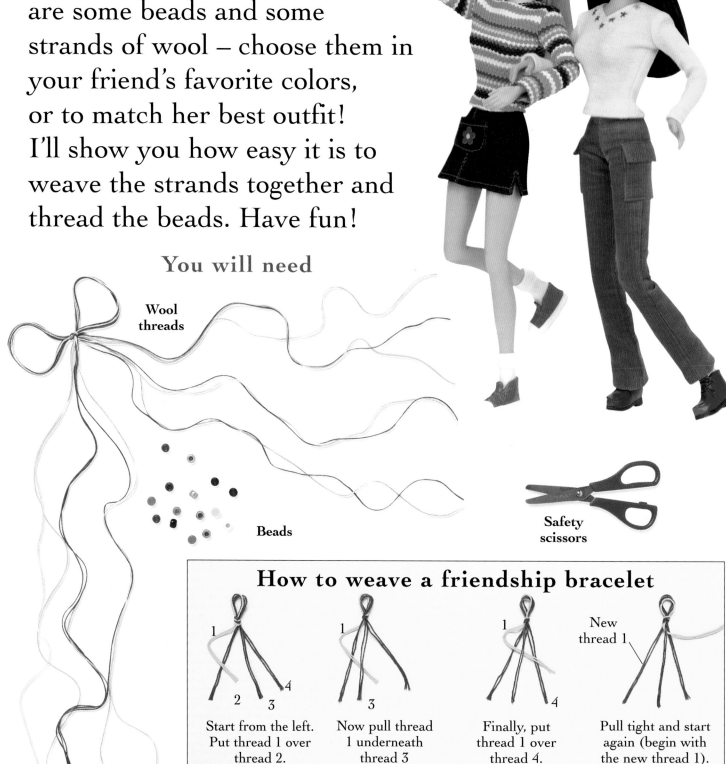

Wool threads

Beads

Safety scissors

How to weave a friendship bracelet

1
2   3   4

Start from the left.
Put thread 1 over
thread 2.

1
3

Now pull thread
1 underneath
thread 3

1
4

Finally, put
thread 1 over
thread 4.

New
thread 1

Pull tight and start
again (begin with
the new thread 1).

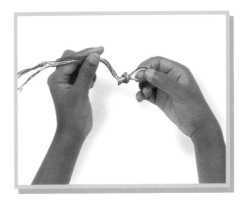

1 Take four colored threads, about 20 in long. Fold them in half; tie a knot in the folded end to make a loop.

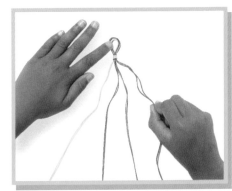

2 Keeping the loop at the top, separate the threads out into their four different colors.

3 Give the loop to your friend to hold. (Or tape the loop to a plastic surface to hold it steady.)

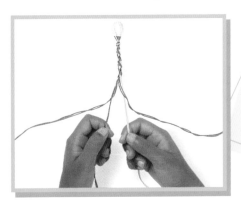

4 Start with the thread on the left. Weave it across the other threads (see box); pull it tight.

Barbie says:
Tie to your friend's wrist by threading the finished end through the loop.

Best of friends!

5 Keep weaving the threads until you are 1 in from the end. Now thread on the beads and knot the ends of thread.

The finished bracelet looks great!

Helpful hints

There are a few extra tips on this page, which will help you with the fun to make activities in this book.

Making holes

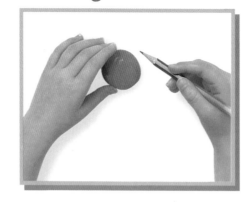

1 You can make holes in paper or card with a ball of modeling clay and a sharp pencil.

2 Put the clay on a table, with the card on top. Press the pencil into the clay, making a neat hole.

Drawing a circle

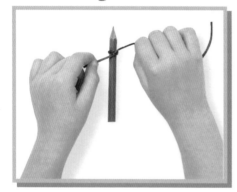

1 Knot a long piece of string tightly around a sharp pencil, just above the tip, as shown.

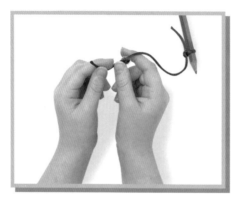

2 For a 4 in circle, put a pin in the string, 2 in (half of 4 in) from the pencil (adapt as needed.)

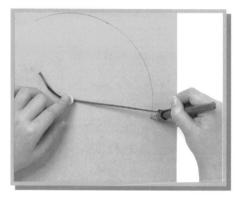

3 Pin the string to some paper. Keep the thread tight as you pull the pencil round in a circle.

Copying patterns

1 Ask a grown-up to photocopy and enlarge the pattern you need, at the required size.

2 Copy the pattern onto tracing paper. Turn the paper over; rub a pencil underneath the outline.

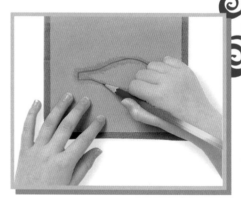

3 Turn back to the traced outline; draw over it again, onto either card or paper, as required.